Shuffle and Squelch

Poems and Rhymes for Children

by **Julia Donaldson**

illustrated by **Nick Sharratt**

MACMILLAN CHILDREN'S BOOKS

For Molly - J.D

For All Saints C of E Junior School - N.S

Poems and illustrations first appeared in *Crazy Mayonnaisy Mum*,
First published 2004 by Macmillan Children's Books,
Shuffle and Squelch published 2015 by Macmillan Children's Books
an imprint of Pan Macmillan
20 New Wharf Road, London N1 9RR
Associated companies throughout the world
www.panmacmillan.com

ISBN: 978-1-4472-7681-4

3 5 7 9 8 6 4 2

A CIP catalogue record for this book is available from the British Library.

Printed in Spain

Contents

Shuffle and Squelch

Spring brings showers; the world's aflood.
Wellies on, let's brave the mud.
We'll go squelching about, squelching about,
Squelching about in the mud,
Yes we'll go squelching about, squelching about,
Squelching about in the mud.

Kick your boots off, everyone.
Summer's here and so's the sun.
We'll go dancing about, dancing about,
Dancing about in the sun,
Yes we'll go dancing about, dancing about,
Dancing about in the sun.

Hold your hat; the winds are thieves.
Watch them steal the autumn leaves
As we shuffle about, shuffle about,
Shuffle about in the leaves,
Yes as we shuffle about, shuffle about,
Shuffle about in the leaves.

Wind your scarf round once or twice.
Winter's turned the world to ice.
We'll go sliding about, sliding about,
Sliding about on the ice,
Yes we'll go sliding about, sliding about,
Sliding about on the ice.

On the Pond in the Park

Splash goes the bread. The ripples spread,
Telling the ducks that it's time to be fed
On the pond
In the park.

Green-headed Dad decides to dine.
Brown-speckled Mum leads the kids in a line
On the pond
In the park.

Go away, goose, you're much too greedy.
Leave a few crumbs for the poor and the needy
On the pond
In the park.

Graceful and white, the long-necked swan
Lets out a hiss and the ducks are all gone
From the pond
In the park.

Cheerio ducks and goodbye drakes.
I'm going home to eat biscuits and cakes
Off a plate
In my house.

Noisy Garden

If tiger lilies and dandelions growled,
And cowslips mooed, and dog roses howled,
And snapdragons roared and catmint miaowed,
My garden would be extremely loud.

Walking the Dog

I take off the lead, open the gate
And watch her run a figure of eight,
And a figure of eight, and a figure of eight,
And another figure of eight.

I walk ten yards along the track
While she goes thundering there and back,
And there and back, and there and back,
And another time there and back.

I settle down upon a log
And watch her chase another dog,
And another dog, and another dog,
And another enormous dog.

I saunter slowly round a lake
While she has a swim and a great big shake,
And a swim and a shake, and a swim and a shake,
And a swim and another big shake.

And now those eyes, that look, that lick
Are begging me to throw a stick,
And throw a stick, and throw a stick,
And the stick, and the very same stick.

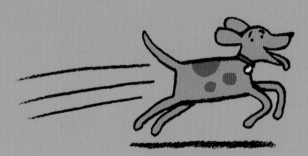

I've walked a mile and she's run ten.
Back home, I flop while she waits again,
And waits again, and waits again
For the W word again.

Buttons

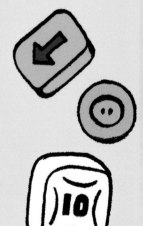

There are coat buttons, shirt buttons,
Cardigan and skirt buttons,
Buttons on the mattress of your bed.
There are loose buttons, tight buttons,
Not-done-up-quite-right buttons,
Buttons that are hanging by a thread.

There are minus and plus buttons,
Let-me-off-the-bus buttons,
Buttons on a fizzy-drinks machine.
There are open-the-door buttons,
Take-me-up-a-floor buttons,
Buttons that can turn the red man green.

There are round buttons, square buttons,
Eyes-on-teddy-bear buttons,
Buttons on a gingerbread man's chest.
But if you're a bit like me
Then I'm sure you will agree
That chocolate buttons are the best.

Pizza

Are you ready? Then off you go.
Punch and pummel that pizza dough.
Roll it out with a rolling pin.
Don't stop rolling till it's nice and thin.

Crush tomatoes and gently spread
Till your pizza is ruby red.
Turn it yellow with grated cheese.
Grind some pepper on but please don't sneeze.

Take a knife and begin to slice.
Pepperoni are pretty nice.
Chop some mushrooms and lots of ham.
Add a pinch or two of marjoram.

Now for seafood, and don't be skimpy.
Make your pizza extremely shrimpy.
Add some mussels, and if you wish
A tin of anchovies or tuna fish.

Mamma mia! You've no idea!
It's the finest pizza in the pizzeria!

Crazy Mayonnaisy Mum

When my friends come home with me
They never want to stay for tea
Because of Mum's peculiar meals
Like strawberries with jellied eels.
You should see her lick her lips
And sprinkle sugar on the chips,
Then pass a cup of tea to you
And ask, 'One salt or two?'

Whoops-a-daisy,
That's my crazy
Mayonnaisy mum.

She serves up ice cream with baked beans,
And golden syrup with sardines,
And curried chocolate mousse on toast,
And once she iced the Sunday roast.
When my birthday comes she'll make
A steak and kidney birthday cake.
There'll be jelly too, of course,
With cheese and onion sauce.

Whoops-a-daisy,
That's my crazy
Mayonnaisy mum.

What's she put in my packed lunch?
A bag of rhubarb crisps to crunch.
Lots of sandwiches as well,
But what is in them? Who can tell?
It tastes like marmalade and ham,
Or maybe fish paste mixed with jam.
What's inside my flask today?
Spinach squash – hooray!

Whoops-a-daisy,
That's my crazy
Mayonnaisy mum.

Luke

Luke liked running round the room.
Luke liked jumping on the bed.
Luke liked splashing in the basin.
What do you think his mother said?

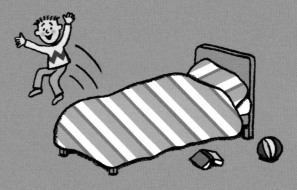

Oh!
Do stop running round the room.
Do stop jumping on the bed.
Do stop splashing in the basin.
Let's go and walk the dog instead.

So
Luke went running round the park.
Luke went jumping off a log.
Luke went splashing in the puddles.
So did his mother and the dog.

Window Cleaner

If you want a cleaner window
Then you want a window cleaner.
You don't want a butcher or a baker or a banker
Or a bowler or a ballerina.
With my ladder nice and steady
And my wiper at the ready
There is no one who is keener
To give you a cleaner window
Than your very own window cleaner.

Two Wheels

I like to look at photographs of me on my old trike.
It had three wheels and never used to wobble like my bike.
Three wheels!
Riding on three wheels!
I used to like riding my trike with three wheels.

Stabilisers made my bike easier to ride.
They stopped it falling over when it tilted to one side.
Four wheels!
Riding on four wheels!
Not quite a bike, not quite a trike, with four wheels.

On the day we took them off, I came off as well,
But now it's great to ride around and tinkle on my bell.
Two wheels!
Riding on two wheels!
That's what I like — riding my bike with two wheels.

Coming Downstairs

My dad comes plodding down the stairs: thump,
thump, thump.

My sister runs down half a flight, then takes a flying
jump.

Our baby comes down backwards, with a slithering
kind of crawl.

My brother tripped the other day and had a nasty
fall.

My mum comes at the gallop. She sounds just like a
horse.

And if you hear a padding sound, why that's the cat
of course.

One step at a time is how Granny comes down
Granny's stairs.

But I don't come downstairs at all — I slide down the
banisters.

There Go the Feet

Horses' hoofs on the cobbles clatter.
Pigeon toes on the pavement patter.
Clatter, patter,
There go the feet.

High-heeled shoes on the floorboards tap.
Divers' flippers on the wet sand flap.
Tap, flap,
Clatter, patter,
There go the feet.

Bedroom slippers on the staircase shuffle.
Football boots on the playing field scuffle.
Shuffle, scuffle,
Tap, flap,
Clatter, patter,
There go the feet.

Ballet pumps on the dance floor trip.
Woolly socks on the lino slip.
Trip, slip,
Shuffle, scuffle,
Tap, flap,
Clatter, patter,
There go the feet.

Rabbits' claws in the burrow scrabble.
Children's toes in the water dabble.
Scrabble, dabble,
Trip, slip,
Shuffle, scuffle,
Tap, flap,
Clatter, patter,
There go the feet.

Elephants' feet in the jungle crash.
Wellington boots in the puddles splash.
Crash, splash,
Scrabble, dabble,
Trip, slip,
Shuffle, scuffle,
Tap, flap,
Clatter, patter,
There go the feet.

Size-one shoes in the playpen toddle.
Ducklings' feet round the duck pond waddle.
Toddle, waddle,
Crash, splash,
Scrabble, dabble,
Trip, slip,
Shuffle, scuffle,
Tap, flap,
Clatter, patter,
THERE GO THE FEET!

Cat Envy

The cat is sleeping on my bed.
She's lucky she can sleep, instead
Of lying worrying all night
And wishing she was black and white
Or wondering why the cat next door
Has stopped being friendly any more.

She sometimes gives herself a groom
But no one makes her clean her room,
And no one's going to wake her up
And yell, 'Bring down that empty cup!'
Or, 'If you don't get moving you'll
Be twenty minutes late for school!'

No wonder she can sleep like that.
I sometimes wish I was the cat.

Guinea Pig

I don't need a tin of cat food
Or toad in the hole for my tea,
But grain I can munch and carrots to crunch,
That's the right kind of food for me.

I don't need a tank to swim in.
I don't want a nest in a tree,
But hay in a hutch I'd like very much.
That's the right kind of home for me.

I don't need a field with cows in:
A pen's big enough to feel free,
With grass I can eat right under my feet.
That's the right kind of space for me.

Please don't rub my fur the wrong way:
Just think and I'm sure you'll agree
That hands which can stroke and don't pinch and poke
Are the right kind of hands for me.

Santa Claws

I don't know why they're blaming me
When all I did was climb a tree
And bat a shiny silver ball.
How could I know the tree would fall?
And when those silly lights went out
They didn't have to scream and shout
And turf me out and shut the door.
Now no one loves me any more.
I'm in the kitchen by myself.
But wait! What's on that high-up shelf?
A lovely turkey, big and fat!
How nice! They do still love their cat.

Riddles

1. I am a lift, a shiny lift,
   With thin white passengers to shift.
   Squeeze them in and send them down.
   When they come up they'll be golden brown.

2. I'm smaller than a mole,
   I'm smaller than a mouse,
   And I turn inside my hole
   When you go into your house.

3. I'm partly red and partly white.
   I have no wings yet I fly through the night.
   I fit in a space that's black and tight.
   I come to you heavy, I go back light.

4. Nippers, grippers, legs in the air.
   The wind may blow but we don't care.
   Nippers, grippers, all in a row.
   Squeeze our legs and we'll let go.

5. I swallow children, women, men.
   I roar and roar and ROAR,
   Then stop and spit them out again
   And swallow up some more.

All the answers can be found in the picture

Cross Katy

Katy didn't want to play,
Not at all, not all day.

'Come on, Katy, let's play tig!'
'No,' said Katy. 'I'm too big.'

'What about a game of ball?'
'No, I don't like that at all.'

'Do you want to climb a tree?'
'You can if you like, not me.'

'Well then, let's play hide and seek.'
'We played that silly game last week.'

'Skipping then? That's good,' I said.
But Katy only shook her head.

So off I went and played with Sue.
Then Katy said, 'Can I play too?'

Fingers and Thumbs

Theo's thumb has wrinkles on it
Because he likes sucking it.

Tammy's tallest finger has a bump on the side of it
Because she likes writing.

Fred's fingertips have hard thick skin
Because he likes playing the guitar.

Aunt Edna's little finger curls in the air when she drinks tea
Because she likes to look elegant.

One of my great-grandmother's fingers has a thimble on it
Because she likes sewing.

Mum's ring finger has a ring on it
Because she likes Dad.

And my fingernails all have dirt under them
Because dirt likes me.

Question Time

How many books have you written?
Have you been writing for years?
Where do you get all the paper?
Where do you get your ideas?

Do you get bumps on your fingers?
Do you get aches in your wrist?
Please can I go to the toilet?
Did you write *Oliver Twist*?

I've got a book about spiders.
I've got a cut on my knee.
I've got an aunt who speaks German.
Gemma keeps tickling me.

Are you quite old? Are you famous?
Are you a millionaire?
I wasn't putting my hand up –
I was just twiddling my hair.

How many plays have you written?
Do you write one every day?
Do you . . . oh dear, I've forgotten
What I was going to say.

Will you be staying to dinner?
Will you go home on the bus?
How many poems have you written?
Will you write one about us?

I Opened a Book

I opened a book and in I strode.
Now nobody can find me.
I've left my chair, my house, my road,
My town and my world behind me.

I'm wearing the cloak, I've slipped on the ring,
I've swallowed the magic potion.
I've fought with a dragon, dined with a king
And dived in a bottomless ocean.

I opened a book and made some friends.
I shared their tears and laughter
And followed their road with its bumps and bends
To the happily ever after.

I finished my book and out I came.
The cloak can no longer hide me.
My chair and my house are just the same,
But I have a book inside me.